Lanie's
Real Adventures

by

Jane Kurtz

★ American Girl®

Questions or comments? Call 1-800-845-0005, visit our Web site at
americangirl.com, or write to Customer Service, American Girl,
8400 Fairway Place, Middleton, WI 53562-0497.

Printed in China
10 11 12 13 14 15 LEO 10 9 8 7 6 5 4 3 2 1

Illustrations by Robert Papp; spot art by Rebecca DeKuiper

Photo credits: pp. 100–101, courtesy Laurel S. Penhale; W.L. Tedders;
pp. 102–103, Bruce Forster; Drake Sorey; pp. 104–105, Michael Ray;
© Amos Nachoum/Corbis

Real Stories/Real Girls stories by Shannon Payette Seip, adapted and
reprinted from *American Girl* magazine

Special thanks to Kathe Crowley Conn

Cataloging-in-Publication Data available from the Library of Congress.

Contents

I crawled out of the tent and shivered as I pulled on my sweatshirt. The cool dawn air smelled fresh and woodsy.

"We're off!" Aunt Hannah whispered so she wouldn't wake the rest of my family, who were still sound asleep in the camper. It was a good thing that Aunt Hannah was sharing my tent. Nobody else in my family likes to be up and out this early. But with the birdsong concert playing in the woods around us, nothing could stop my aunt and me.

At the trailhead, I spotted my very first red-winged blackbird. Ooh-la-la! The twenty-third bird on my bird-watcher's Life List. I watched the bird for a moment, planning exactly how I would draw those shiny black wings and splats of red in my field notes.

"Listen," Aunt Hannah said suddenly.

A loud and lively chirping bubbled from the tree branches above our heads. Number twenty-four for my Life List?

Factoid

There are close to 10,000 species of birds in the world. I want to see as many of them as I can!

I scrambled onto a stump. Looking through my binoculars, I could see the bird's outline against the sky.

"Any clues?" Aunt Hannah asked.

"Nope," I said after a minute. "I can't make it out. Too far away."

Aunt Hannah's face had a fierce-concentration look. "Even though it's far away, it's really loud. That makes me think it's a Carolina wren. Just think—its vocal cords would fit in a raindrop, but no wren within a quarter of a mile is going to miss *that* message."

"What *is* the message?"

"He's saying, 'This is *my* oak tree and *my* nest and *my* sunrise.'" Aunt Hannah jumped up and down and waved her fists. "'All mine, mine, mine—so you'd better stay out.'"

I laughed and then gave her an *I'm-not-as-great-as-I-thought-I-was* face. "Darn, I thought I knew what Carolina wrens sounded like."

"Don't feel bad. Male Carolina wrens have at least thirty different songs."

"Oh." I hopped down from the stump. "That's a lot."

We walked in silence a bit longer, taking in all the early-morning bird chatter, and then started back to the campsite for breakfast. I took Aunt Hannah's hand.

"This is my favorite day this whole summer," I said.

She squeezed. "Mine too."

"Really? Even better than when you were recording bellbird songs in Costa Rica?"

She grinned at me. "Well, Costa Rica *was* pretty awesome. It had some amazing birds." She paused. "But it didn't have you."

A warm syrup of happiness spread in my chest. Aunt Hannah is the best.

It was a record day for me: I added four new birds to my bird-watcher's Life List. I spotted raccoon tracks in the mud near the bank of a pond. I saw my first-ever red-spotted newt. And I got a huge blister on  my heel from so much hiking. After that, Mom made me sit and soak my feet in a pan of cold water while she helped Dad cook dinner.

My little sister, Emily, was fascinated by my blister.

"Can I see it again?" she asked.

I pulled my foot out of the water.

"Ooh, it looks like a big bubble under your skin. Can I touch it?"

I'd had such a great day, I was feeling generous. "Sure, go ahead."

"Eww, it's gross!"

"It's just a blister, Emily." I felt rather proud of it. It was like a badge of honor. Proof that I'd spent the day outdoors, hiking and exploring.

After poking my blister one more time, Emily zipped off to play checkers inside the camper with our big sister, Angela. As Emily pulled the camper's screen door shut behind her, I fluttered my feet in the water and wondered for the hundredth time how we could be so different and yet still be sisters. I mean, why would they prefer to be inside the camper with all this awesome nature all around us?

My hypothesis: my sisters—like my parents—were born with inside genes. Their species doesn't quite get the joy of being outdoors. Aunt Hannah and I, on the other hand, were born with outside genes. We like to soak up every outdoors moment possible.

Proof of my hypothesis: *They* prefer sleeping in Aunt Hannah's camper, while Aunt Hannah prefers to sleep outside in a tent with me.

Still, I think there's hope for Emily. She likes watching birds in the backyard with me, and at the end of the school year, when her class was hatching monarch butterflies, she got so interested that she even overcame her bug phobia. And she loves helping me sketch wildlife in our nature journal. She might have a few outside genes after all.

When my toes were as wrinkled as prunes, I carefully dried my feet with a towel and then slipped into my flip-flops. Mom sat down on the log beside me and handed me a small metal cup filled with lemonade. It was so tart that my mouth puckered at the first taste.

"Did Dad make this?" I asked when I could finally talk.

She nodded. "It's a fresh-squeezed lemon, but he forgot to pack sugar or honey. All he had to sweeten it were a few little sugar packets that Hannah had in her camper for her coffee."

"It's not too bad, once you get used to it." My parents had taken this camping trip for me, so I was determined to be positive about every part of it, even the sour parts. "You know, I think Dad likes cooking outside over an open fire. I hope we can go camping again soon, don't you?"

"Well, it's certainly an adventure, but you have

to admit it's a bit strange to actually *enjoy* sleeping on the hard ground, hiking until you get blisters, washing your hair in cold water, and keeping your garbage can locked so that raccoons don't come snooping." Mom smiled at me. "I guess I don't completely understand outside girls like you and Hannah."

"Come on, Mom," I said. "Don't criticize my species."

She laughed. I did, too.

That night after dinner, we sat around the campfire, and Emily and I toasted marshmallows. The flickering flames and the eerie hooting of an owl sent happy chills up my spine. Then I heard a familiar sound— Angela was tuning her cello. At first I had been annoyed when she insisted on bringing it along on our trip. A cello on a camping trip? It just seemed all wrong. I mean, a cello is not exactly in the spirit of roughing it outdoors. But now, with the campfire coals glowing and the soft strains of the cello and the stars sparkling in the purple-black sky, it was truly magical. I had to admit, I was glad Angela had brought the cello along. Maybe indoor things and outdoor things aren't complete opposites after all.

By the time we got home the next day, it was too late to do anything but give Lulu, my lop-eared rabbit, an I'm-glad-to-see-you-again brushing. Then I clicked on my laptop to see if my best friend, Dakota, had e-mailed me. Part of me hoped she had, but part of me hoped she hadn't—because that might mean she was already on a plane heading home to me!

Dakota's been in Indonesia, where her dad is studying the rain forest. When she first left, I missed her horribly. Then, when she started sending pictures of herself with baby orangutans, I felt even more horrible— horribly *envious*. Dakota has all the luck. In her family, they do awesome things like going off to live in a jungle for six months, while in my family, it's a miracle that we even went on a three-day camping trip.

As my laptop powered up, an orangutan picture bloomed onto the screen—a photo from Dakota that I was using as my computer wallpaper. The picture was adorable . . .

. . . Dakota and I are tramping through the rain forest. Brightly colored birds fly from tree to tree. Dakota points through the misty green world— a young orangutan is up in the tree ahead. It clings to branches using its hands and feet . . .

Ping. I had e-mail.

From: Dakota <dakotanotthestate@4natr.net>
Date: June 25, 2010 5:41 P.M.
To: Lanie <hollandnotthecountry@4natr.net>
Subject: School's out!!

   Hey! School is finally out, but I've been busier than ever volunteering at the orangutan center. We're coming home, but not quite as soon as we thought. There are some problems here and we're trying to help. Oops, I have to go now. I miss u!

I had been dying to tell Dakota all about my camping trip, but as usual my life seemed boring and trivial next to hers. I was also a little worried, because it sounded like something serious was happening.

From: Lanie <hollandnotthecountry@4natr.net>
To: Dakota <dakotanotthestate@4natr.net>
Date: June 27, 2010 8:12 P.M.
Subject: Re: School's out!!

   So what's going on there? What are the problems you're having? Are you okay? Are the orangutans okay? Please tell me more as soon as you can. I miss u too. P.S. When are you coming home?

The next morning, the intercom buzzed in my room, startling me awake. My mom's an architect, and when she redesigned our house, she installed an intercom. That might seem odd, but it's actually very handy. I slid over and pushed the button. "Mom?"

Emily's voice floated into my room. "Lanie! It's me. Come down to the deck—you've got to see this!"

I pulled on clean sweatpants and zipped up my sweatshirt from yesterday. It still smelled nice and smoky from the campfire. Remembering my blister, I grabbed my flip-flops and hurried downstairs, through the kitchen and onto the deck. By the side of the house, Aunt Hannah was coming out of her camper, coffee mug in hand. She's staying in the camper in our backyard for a few months, until she can move into university housing when she starts graduate school this fall.

Emily grabbed my hand. "Look!" She pointed to the plum tree next to the deck.

I walked over to see what she was looking at. In the crook of the tree, where the trunk divided into three branches, was a messy collection of sticks and grass and leaves and scraps of paper. "A nest!" Emily cried. "Right, Aunt Hannah? Am I right?"

"You are right," said Aunt Hannah, joining us on the deck. "Good eye, Emily!" Emily beamed. "Now, here's a challenge—there are no eggs, so how do we know what kind of bird built this nest?"

"We don't," said Emily, logically.

"We'll have to wait until the bird gets back, and *then* we'll know," I answered. Emily isn't the only logical thinker in our family.

"That would be one way to tell," Aunt Hannah agreed. "But we don't have to wait for the bird to come back—we can use other clues. Here's the first clue: most birds are particular about what kinds of materials they use to build their nests, and they build nice neat nests. But not Carolina wrens—they use all kinds of nest-building materials, so their nests can look rather messy."

"Maybe they look messy to us but probably not to the wrens," I pointed out.

"Good point, Lanie!" Aunt Hannah grinned at me, and my chest swelled with pride. "Clue number two—Carolina wrens often build a new nest and lay a second brood in July. Clue number three—we've seen Carolina wrens in the yard before, so we know they're in this area."

Emily started hopping up and down with

excitement. "So if the bird lays some eggs, we'll have baby wrens right in our yard. We'll be able to watch them from the deck!"

Of course we didn't want to bother a female bird sitting on eggs, but Aunt Hannah said it was okay to look around and keep our ears open. She said the mama would chatter at us if we got too close, so we should listen for that. "It's also possible that the male wren will start singing," she added.

"Why?" asked Emily.

"To tell us, 'This is *my* house—stay away!'" Then Aunt Hannah suggested we all sit on the deck and try listening.

I tried to focus my thoughts, but after a while my mind drifted into a daydream . . .

> . . . *Aunt Hannah and I are tramping through the Costa Rican cloud forest. An emerald toucanet squawks, and bright hummingbirds whiz by our heads, but we're hoping to hear a bellbird, with its strange call—*

Tea kettle, tea kettle, tea kettle!
Wait a minute. That's not how the bellbird sounds—

The Harsh Truth

Aunt Hannah jumped up, almost spilling her coffee.

"There. There. There!" Emily jumped up and down, pointing.

The wren was on top of the roof of the garden shed at the back of our yard. Was it my imagination, or was it puffing out its chest and trying to act like the biggest, baddest wren on the block?

"That's the male wren, all right," Aunt Hannah said. "I wonder where the female is?"

A movement caught the corner of my eye. I turned. Caesar, the big orange cat that lives next door, was strolling into our yard like he owned the place. I looked back at the nest in the plum tree. Suddenly, a few feet from the deck at eye level didn't seem like such a great place for a nest. All Caesar would have to do was hop onto our deck railing, and from there it was one short leap into the plum tree.

My eyes met Aunt Hannah's, and I knew she was thinking the same thing. The wrens needed a safer place for their home.

"Emily, we're going to have to take down this nest," Aunt Hannah said gently.

"No!" Emily looked shocked. "The wrens want to lay their eggs there!"

"I know," Aunt Hannah told her. "That's the problem."

I could see she was trying to avoid upsetting Emily, but Emily didn't understand, and that was just making her more upset. It was up to me to tell my little sister the harsh truth.

I pointed at Caesar. "That cat could get to the nest easily. The baby birds would be helpless." Emily looked at me in horror. "We wouldn't want that, would we?" I asked, and she shook her head.

"We'll just move this nest to a higher branch of the tree, where the cat can't reach," said Aunt Hannah. "I don't know whether the wrens will come back to it, but it's worth a try. I'll get a ladder."

We did our best. Aunt Hannah hauled the ladder out of the garage, set it up on the deck, and climbed up. I lifted the wren's nest as carefully as I could, but a few sticks fell out and it felt sort of wobbly in my hand, as if it might collapse. I handed it to Aunt Hannah, and she set it in the fork of a high, thin branch of the plum tree.

"We'll keep an eye on it and see if the wrens return," she told us. She folded up the ladder and took it back to the garage.

The Harsh Truth

I glared at Caesar, who sat placidly on the grass, watching us with his green eyes. "This is all your fault," I informed him. "Those wrens had a perfectly nice home and, because of you, we had to mess it up."

Caesar turned and stalked back into his yard. He sat down under a rosebush and began to lick his fur.

Caesar belongs to Ms. Marshall, our next-door neighbor. She moved in a few months ago, back in the spring. Ms. Marshall has a perfectly manicured lawn surrounded by rows and rows of perfectly pruned roses. Her lawn does not have one single dandelion in it. She had not been too happy when Aunt Hannah, Emily, and I had torn up *our* lawn and planted milk-weed and prairie plants to attract monarchs and other butterflies. It's true that our plantings don't look like much yet—just tall, spindly plants growing here and there in no particular order.

Okay, to be honest, they *do* kind of look like weeds, especially in comparison to her elegant rose-bushes. But Aunt Hannah had explained that our wild-flowers would really take off in July and start blooming, and then they would be pretty. Unfortunately, that doesn't help right now.

"What's going to happen when all those seeds start blowing into my yard?" our neighbor had asked.

I wanted to tell her that monarch butterflies need milkweed to survive. I had learned about this last spring when I helped Emily's class with their butterfly project. I had also learned that Ms. Marshall really likes monarchs. Probably for the same reason she likes roses— because they're so pretty. But milkweed plants, which monarch caterpillars eat, are not pretty, at least not in the normal way. They're pale green, with thick stalks and just a few coarse leaves. Still, they're beautiful to me, now that I know how important they are. Without milkweed, there would be no monarchs.

Besides, milkweed wasn't the only thing we'd planted in our new wild backyard. Adult monarchs don't eat milkweed; they only sip nectar. So we had planted plenty of nectar-producing flowers. I liked their names: black-eyed Susan, blazing star, butterfly weed, purple coneflower, bee balm, goldenrod. They're all native plants, just like milkweed. Aunt Hannah had shown me a picture of a natural garden with these kinds of flowers all blooming, and it was breathtaking, with blossoms of every color. But it was very different from the orderly rows of roses marching across Ms. Marshall's yard.

A screen door slammed, and Ms. Marshall came out onto her patio. I usually see her dressed for work, wearing high heels and dress suits, but today she had on khakis and a crisp blouse and gardening gloves. She carried a spray bottle in each hand. As I watched her from behind the deck railing, she began walking slowly around her lawn. Every now and then, she would pause and spray a spot with one of her spray bottles. Then she walked over to her roses and started spraying them.

Curiosity got the better of me. I left the safety of my deck and walked to the edge of our lawn. "Hi, Ms. Marshall," I said brightly, hoping that I sounded friendlier than I felt.

"Oh, hello, Lanie," she replied.

"Um, what are you spraying?"

She held up her two bottles. "This one is an herbicide, for dandelions. And this one's a pesticide, to keep insects off my roses. The flower buds are about to open, so I don't want to risk having them damaged by aphids."

"Aphids? What are those?" I asked. I couldn't imagine anything wanting to eat her spiky, thorny rosebushes. They didn't look tender and munchable, like our baby milkweed plants.

"Come here and I'll show you," Ms. Marshall said, waving me into her yard.

I went over, and she pointed to a rose leaf that

looked sort of curled back on itself. She uncurled the leaf and turned it over, and I could see a patch of tiny greenish-gray bumps on the underside.

"Those little things could hurt your roses?" I asked.

"Yes. They may be small, but aphids suck the plant juice out of the leaf. It doesn't take many aphids to wilt a leaf or a flower bud. A bad infestation can kill the whole plant, although roses are pretty tough. But just a few aphids can easily ruin the flower buds." She gave the green bumps a squirt from her spray bottle. "That should take care of them," she said with satisfaction.

After breakfast, I fired up my laptop and went to the Monarch Watch Web site. Aunt Hannah had shown me how I could fill out a form to certify our backyard as an official Monarch Waystation.

Factoid

Every year, monarchs migrate 2,000 miles, from the U.S. and Canada all the way to Mexico—and back again.

Imagine, fragile little butterflies flying all the way to Mexico and back! For a long time, scientists had no idea where the monarchs went in the fall. Then they discovered that the monarchs actually hibernate in trees! Zillions of them cover whole trees and sleep through the winter. In the spring, they wake up and return home to lay their eggs on milkweed plants.

Milkweed is what the monarch caterpillars eat. In areas where milkweed has disappeared, so have the monarchs. When people build roads, houses, and lawns, milkweed gets destroyed. Even farms and cropland take away milkweed habitat. So to help the monarchs, some people are starting to plant milkweed on their property. Scientists keep track of these monarch-friendly places. They want to know where monarchs are living and breeding, so that they can study them and monitor the health of the species.

I had filled out most of the Monarch Waystation form a while ago:

Name: Monarch Heaven
Type: suburban
Location: backyard
Size: about 150 square feet
Milkweeds: Common Milkweed
Plant Density:

This last line was still blank, because we weren't sure how many of our new backyard milkweed plants would make it. For a while it hadn't looked too good, because milkweed is a slow grower. But finally the young plants had taken off, and now they looked healthy and inviting. I could hardly wait for a female monarch to flutter over them and think, *Finally—after such a long journey, a delicious place to lay my eggs.*

Now that our milkweed plants were growing big and strong, Emily and I had been able to count them. We had about twelve milkweeds growing. I checked my notes and typed, *1–2 milkweed plants per square yard,* and then clicked *Submit.*

My backyard was now an official Monarch Waystation. Scientists would be collecting and using the data from my very own backyard! That is, if any monarchs ever showed up.

I sighed. Twelve milkweed plants didn't seem like very much. Each caterpillar eats milkweed almost nonstop until it turns into a butterfly, and I knew from helping feed the caterpillars in Emily's class last spring that they go through a lot of milkweed. I wanted to have more milkweed—a lot more, so that we'd have lots of caterpillars turning into strong, healthy monarchs. But where could we plant more? Between the pizza garden and the wildflower garden, our whole backyard was used up.

Suddenly I had a brainstorm: what about the *front* yard? Dad was always complaining about having to mow the lawn every week. We used to have a noisy, smelly gas-powered mower, but a few years ago Dad replaced it with a push mower. It was quieter and didn't stink, but it was harder work for Dad—he always said he couldn't wait until I was big enough to do the mowing with my outdoor genes. He was delighted when we dug up the backyard to plant vegetables and wildflowers, and he didn't have to mow it anymore. Now I could save him from mowing the front lawn, too!

I ran downstairs to tell everyone my great idea.

A few hours later, I was outside in the front yard with a shovel. Aunt Hannah had laid a tarp on the driveway, and we were digging up clods of lawn and dumping them onto the tarp. Now and then, we would stop and gather the four corners of the tarp and drag it into our backyard, where we dumped the dirt-and-grass clods onto the compost pile. Every so often, Mom or Dad would come to the front window and give us a thumbs-up. After a few hours, my back was sore and my hands were aching, but we had a nice smooth bed of rich brown earth all ready to plant.

Aunt Hannah came out of the house with her purse over her shoulder. "Let's drive to the garden center and get some seeds and starter plants."

Now that the work was done, the fun could begin. I'd never paid much attention to our front yard before. It looked just like all the other front yards on the block— just a small lawn with a few bushes on either side of the front porch, nothing special. Kind of boring, to be honest. But now it was going to be a beautiful wildflower garden, full of butterflies and birds. I could hardly wait!

The next morning, we were all eating breakfast when the doorbell rang. Emily and I raced to answer it. Our neighbor, Ms. Marshall, was standing on our front porch. A funny feeling fluttered in my stomach. She had never come over to our house before. "Um, hi, Ms. Marshall," I said. "How are your aphids?"

"Dead, I hope. I just noticed your—your new front yard. Um, what are your plans for that, if I may ask?" Her smile seemed a bit stiff.

Emily spoke up. "Dad doesn't like mowing our lawn," she informed Ms. Marshall.

"I see. Did he consider hiring someone to do it for him?"

I shook my head. "Emily's right, but that's not why we dug up the lawn." I told her about my plans for more milkweed and wildflowers, so that the monarchs would have more habitat. As I talked, the stiff smile on her face faded. Feeling nervous, I started explaining about the monarchs' big migration, but she cut me short.

"Are your parents home?"

Emily and I nodded. Just then, Mom came to the door.

"Mrs. Holland, I don't mean to be unfriendly, but your front yard is now as big an eyesore as your backyard, and quite frankly, it's not fair to your neighbors."

"It'll be pretty when the plants get big, honest," I tried to tell her.

"The ones in your backyard *are* getting big, and they still look like weeds—because they *are* weeds."

"No, they're not—"

"Yes, they are. You said so yourself."

"*Milk*weed," I clarified. "That's different."

"Weeds are weeds," Ms. Marshall said in a no-nonsense tone. "This is a lovely, traditional neighborhood, and between the weeds and that trailer parked in your driveway, your property is now a real eyesore. Not only that, but your weed seeds will spread to your neighbors' yards and create trouble for everyone. I'm going to have to talk to some of the other neighbors. I think they'll agree this is going too far, and we need to put a stop to it."

Before Mom could say anything, Ms. Marshall turned on her high heel and left.

I ran up to my room, picked up Lulu, and buried my face in her fur. She seemed to know I needed a friend and snuggled her nose into the crook of my elbow, her favorite spot.

It was times like these that I really missed my best friend. I put Lulu down and switched on my laptop. Good old Dakota—an e-mail was waiting for me.

From: Dakota <dakotanotthestate@4natr.net>
Date: June 29, 2010 6:59 P.M.
To: Lanie <hollandnotthecountry@4natr.net>
Subject: orangutans & trees

   Here's what's going on. People in this region
have been cutting down trees in the forest where
the orangutans live. The people here are poor, and
they need the trees for lumber and firewood. A tree
is valuable and sells for a lot of money. But the
orangutans need the trees to live. Without trees,
they can't eat or sleep or hide. It's a real problem.
We're trying to help, but it's hard to know what to do.

Wow. If I thought it was sad thinking about
monarchs without enough milkweed to eat, what about
orangutans without enough trees? I didn't even know
what to say. I had been planning to tell Dakota about
our horrible neighbor, but as usual, my life didn't seem
nearly as interesting as hers. Even my problems seemed
less important.

There was a tap on my door, and Mom poked
her head into my room. "Lanie, may I come in?"

I nodded, and she sat down on my bed. "So,"
she began, "it sounds like our new neighbor is pretty
unhappy about our yard."

I frowned. "Mom, she doesn't understand! Wild-flowers like these just take a while to get going. Aunt Hannah says they really put on a show in July, and it's nearly the end of June—"

"I know, honey. But it's a different kind of gardening—a different kind of beauty," said Mom. "Different people appreciate different things. I see this when I design homes for people. What one client thinks is the most beautiful house in the world looks hideous to another client."

"But don't we have the right to plant whatever we want on our own property?"

Mom paused, looking thoughtful. "When you live in a community with other people, you have to get along with your neighbors. We own our separate houses, but we all share the neighborhood. And even if we might have the *legal* right to do something, that doesn't necessarily make it okay, if it offends those around us."

"Does this mean we have to put the lawn back?" I hoped not, because that could be a problem. "I think it's kind of wrecked—we'd have to plant new grass seed."

"Or how about planting some roses? I'll bet Ms. Marshall would be fine with that." Mom winked to let me know she was kidding.

"But Mom, seriously, what am I supposed to do?"

"What do you *want* to do, Lanie?"

I knew the answer to that. "I want to have good habitat for monarchs." I showed Mom the sheet I'd printed out from the Monarch Watch Web site, stating that our yard was now an official Monarch Waystation.

Mom looked impressed. "Monarch Heaven, huh?" She smiled. "I'm proud of you, Lanie. This is important. But it's also important to live in harmony with our neighbors. So if you don't want to give up your garden goals—and I do think they're very worthwhile goals— then you'll have to find a way to help Ms. Marshall see things your way."

"But Mom, how am I going to do that?"

She gave me a smile. "That's a toughie, isn't it?"

"Lanie!" Aunt Hannah was calling me. "Are you ready to go?"

Before school ended, I had signed up for a summertime young gardener project run by my fourth-grade teacher, Mr. James. I wanted to learn more about gardening, and Aunt Hannah had offered to come along and help out.

Emily poked her head into my room. "Why are you gardening somewhere else? Isn't our pizza garden enough?"

Last spring, to get Emily more interested in spending time outside, she and Dad and I had planted a pizza garden—a big circle of pizza ingredients like tomatoes, basil, oregano, peppers, zucchini, and onions. Emily had inspired the idea, because pizza was the only thing she ever ate. And it had worked! Now she loved being in our backyard as much as I did.

"Do we need more pizza food?" Emily asked.

"No," I told her. "This garden isn't for us to eat from. It's to help kids learn more about gardening." I stood up and shut off my laptop.

"Can I come?"

"Sorry, Emily. It's for fourth- and fifth-graders." Emily looked disappointed, and I felt a little sorry for her. "Maybe I can take you there some other time, when it's not during the gardening class."

As Aunt Hannah and I drove to the community gardens, I was quiet. I could see my aunt glancing at me out of the corner of her eye. Finally she asked, "Everything okay, Lanie?"

I told Aunt Hannah what Ms. Marshall had said about how our yard was an eyesore in the neighborhood, and how Mom had said it was important to live in harmony with our neighbors. I left out the part about the camper being an eyesore, too.

"When you have a neighbor like yours, that's a challenge." Aunt Hannah looked sympathetic. "I'm glad we're doing this today, Lanie. It'll be good for you to have a change of scene and get together with some friends." She turned the car in to the parking lot.

Even though they're as different as sisters can be, sometimes Aunt Hannah sounds just like my mother.

We climbed out, and she opened her trunk. From a box she handed me a milk jug that had its top cut off and was half-full of soapy water.

"What is this for?" I asked.

"Dunking squash bugs."

She picked up two more and we carried them, sloshing and trying not to spill, across the parking lot. As we got closer, we could see about thirty or forty garden plots with narrow paths between them. Lots of people, both grown-ups and kids, were hoeing or pulling weeds. At one end of the gardens were a park and ball fields. At the other end, a long weedy strip of land separated the gardens from a rocky outcrop. In the distance, Boston's tall buildings were visible above the trees.

"Do you see your teacher?" Aunt Hannah asked.

I looked around and spotted Mr. James with a group of kids around my age. I recognized some of them from school, but nobody I was really friends with. I was sort of surprised to see that there were so many kids interested in gardening.

"Hi, Lanie. How nice to see you on this beautiful summer morning!" Mr. James called, waving at me.

I waved back, and we walked over to the group. "Hi, Mr. James. This is my Aunt Hannah. She wanted to come along and help out." I added, "She's studying to be an ornithologist." That means bird scientist. I hoped Mr. James would be impressed that I had used such a scientific word. And that I had an aunt who was a real scientist.

Aunt Hannah held up her milk jugs. "I brought some nontoxic pest control, in case we need it."

"Good idea," said Mr. James.

Nicholas

A boy from my fourth-grade class stuck his finger into the milk jug solution and let it drip off. "What is this stuff?" he asked.

"Soapy water. It's to get rid of squash bugs and eggs on cucumber, squash, and melon leaves," Aunt Hannah explained.

Mr. James nodded.

"How does it work?" asked a girl.

"Like this." Aunt Hannah walked over to a zucchini plant, turned over a few leaves, picked up a small beetle, and dropped it into the milk jug. Even though I knew it was better for the garden, I couldn't help feeling a tiny bit sorry for the beetle.

"You mean we have to touch the bugs?" the girl asked, wrinkling her nose.

"My dad sprays some chemical stuff on his flowers to get rid of the bugs," said a boy.

"Pesticides are actually poison," Mr. James told him. "People are going to *eat* our vegetables, remember? So we don't want to put poison on them."

Aunt Hannah nodded. "Pesticides will take care of squash bugs, but they also hurt helpful insects like ladybugs and lacewings, which eat pests, and bees, which pollinate plants. So it's better not to use pesticides, even if you're just growing flowers. You can't control which plants the bees visit." She handed the boy a milk jug before he could say no.

Wait a minute. That stuff that my neighbor was spraying on her roses? That was pesticide—*poison*. Right next door to my monarch habitat!

Mr. James pointed out a few of the most common weeds we were concentrating on pulling—dandelions, broadleaf plantains, and thistles. "Help yourselves to tools and gloves from that pile there," he told us. "Then pick an area and start weeding!"

A boy with shaggy brown hair was weeding by one of the tomato plants. I recognized him as a fifth-grader from my school.

"Hey, Nicholas. Can I weed here with you?" I asked. He glanced up at me, and then shrugged and turned back to his weeding.

Not exactly a friendly welcome. So much for Aunt Hannah's idea of me getting together with friends here.

With a sigh, I plopped down between two huge tomato plants and pulled on my gloves. For a while, I enjoyed the satisfaction of the weeds' roots sliding out of the dirt. When I got tired of that, I escaped into a daydream . . .

Nicholas

. . . I'm in Africa, trudging through the long grass,
keeping an eye out for chimpanzees. Suddenly I
spot one by a tall, narrow mound of dirt—a termite
mound. The chimp pokes a stick into the mound,
pulls it out, and puts it in his mouth, slurping
the termites off . . .

I sighed and tossed a dandelion into my weed
bucket. Thinking about chimpanzees made me think
about orangutans, and thinking about orangutans made
me sad. Better switch to something happier—like the
monarch butterflies that were going to migrate through
Boston any day now and start laying eggs on the milkweed plants in our backyard.

Monarchs are truly remarkable. Few living creatures can navigate over such long distances as migrating
monarchs. And the really amazing thing is that the
monarchs that fly south in the fall *have never been there*
before. They are the great-great-grandchildren of the
ones that flew north the previous spring. Unlike birds,
they don't have experienced parents along to guide them.
None of them have ever made the trip, yet somehow they
know exactly where to go.

It must have been thrilling to be one of the
scientists who first discovered a monarch tree . . .

. . . I'm hiking in the mountains of northern Mexico, between tall fir trees. The bark of the trees has an odd texture. Suddenly I realize that the entire trunk is completely covered with the folded wings of millions of butterflies, all sleeping close together to keep warm . . .

"Did you know that a blue whale's tongue can weigh as much as an elephant?"

I blinked and looked up from my weeding. Did I miss something?

"Hello! Earth to Lanie." Nicholas was talking to me.

"Sorry, did you say something about a—a blue whale?"

"Forget it." He turned away again.

"Wait—did you say that its tongue weighs as much as an elephant?" That sounded like a factoid to me.

He shrugged. "Yeah. They both weigh around four tons. Most people don't realize that."

I shook the dirt out of a big clump of roots, impressed. Suddenly I thought of a good one. "Did you know that the state soil of Massachusetts has a name?"

He narrowed his eyes, thinking. I expected him

to shrug again and look away, but instead he turned to me and raised his eyebrows. I saw a spark of interest— and challenge.

"Paxton," I told him. "Kind of weird, huh?"

He grinned.

Something was crawling on my arm—a ladybug. Gently I picked it off my arm and set it on a tomato leaf. There was a tiny drop of yellow fluid on my arm where the ladybug had been.

"I think a ladybug just peed on me," I announced.

Nicholas peered at my arm. "Nah. It's just a little fluid that comes out of its leg joints. That's how the ladybug defends itself."

"It kind of stinks."

"It was probably an Asian lady beetle," Nicholas said. "They're a lot smellier. Scientists think they might be crowding out the native species."

"What are you, a ladybug-ologist?"

Nicholas shrugged. "Did you know that the ladybug is the official state insect of Massachusetts?" Then, taking off his gloves, he pulled a folded-up piece of paper from his pocket and handed it to me.

I opened it up. It was a tattered newspaper article with a photo of a boy who looked just like— "Is that you? In *The Boston Globe*?" I asked.

He nodded. "I found a C-9. That's a nine-spotted ladybug." Nicholas pointed at the article. "The native ladybugs around here usually have two spots. I like looking for ones with more. Nine-spotted ones are really rare. In fact, mine was only the second nine-spotted ladybug found in the eastern United States in fourteen years. Scientists had thought they might be extinct, so they were excited, and it got into the newspaper."

"Hey, let's find some more ladybugs and count their spots!" Going on that kind of treasure hunt sounded way more fun than weeding. Our section of the tomato patch was pretty much done, anyway. I was ready for a break.

Step one was to find a ladybug. You'd think it would be easy, since ladybugs are so common, but now that we were looking for them, they were playing hide-and-seek with us. I squatted down, gently pushing through the leaves, looking for a little red or orange beetle. Suddenly I spotted one. Carefully, I put my thumbnail in front of it and let it walk onto my hand. Maybe I would get lucky on my first try! But it had only two spots.

"I got one," said Nicholas. "Seven spots."

"What do we do if we find one with nine spots?"

"Well, we'd need to get a photo of it. So we would

catch it and put it in a cooler with ice for a few minutes, and then we'd snap a photo."

"Why in a cooler with ice?"

"The cold slows the ladybug down enough so that you can get the photo. It doesn't hurt the ladybug— as long as you don't leave it in very long. You can do it with other insects, too. And with butterflies."

Was there anything this kid didn't know about ladybugs?

After another fifteen minutes of hunting, we had found several more ladybugs, but none of them had nine spots. Nicholas was much better at finding them than I was, so I let him do the hunting while I went back to weeding. I told him about how my yard was an official Monarch Waystation and was going to be part of the famous monarch migration. I didn't mention that my neighbor was on the warpath because of my garden.

Nicholas was interested and asked me a lot of questions, which made me feel good. "A monarch way-station—that's cool, Lanie. Seriously, very cool."

I smiled at him. "Would you like to come over and see it?"

He broke into a grin. "Definitely! How about this Thursday?"

I nodded happily. Finally, someone who could appreciate my scientific efforts.

Later, as we drove home, it occurred to me that maybe Aunt Hannah did know a thing or two about kids after all.

When we got home, Emily was waiting for us.

"Dinner's almost ready," she announced.

"Great—I'm starving," I said. "What is Dad cooking?"

"Lemonade."

"What? Dad's making lemonade for *dinner*?"

"That's what he said." Emily shrugged. "It does have lemons in it, but it doesn't look like lemonade."

Aunt Hannah and I exchanged a glance. "Let's get to the bottom of this," she murmured.

My father is famous in our family for his mystery dishes. I love his jalapeno jelly pizza, but I had skipped the corn ice cream he made once—I mean, *corn ice cream*? But this time, when we arrived in the kitchen, a delicious aroma greeted us.

"Ah, you're just in time for dinner," he told us, looking up from the sauté pan he was stirring. "The angel hair's almost done."

"We're having hair in our lemonade?" Emily asked, her blue eyes wide.

Dad, Aunt Hannah, and I tried to stifle our laughter. "Not lemonade, Emily—*gremolade*," said Dad.

I turned to Aunt Hannah. "What's that?"

"I have no idea," she replied, and we laughed again.

"Whatever it is, it smells good, anyway," Mom said, joining us in the kitchen.

"I'm making sautéed spring vegetables with gremolade, which is parsley, lemon zest, and garlic. The baby zucchini and carrots came out of our garden," Dad said proudly. "And angel hair is pasta."

I'm not crazy about vegetables, but I had to admit these tasted great.

"Nothing like fresh garden vegetables, picked only a few hours ago, to change your mind forever about eating veggies," said Aunt Hannah.

After dinner, Emily and I went out onto the deck to see if the wrens had returned to the nest we'd moved. We couldn't hear any bird chatter, so Aunt Hannah hauled the ladder back out to take a look inside.

"Empty," she reported. Emily's face fell. "It could take them a day or two to find it, though," Aunt Hannah added. "We'll keep checking."

The next day I asked Aunt Hannah about her soap recipe for squash bugs. "Would it work on aphids, too?" I asked.

Aunt Hannah raised her eyebrows. "Did you

find aphids on any of our garden plants?"

"No, but Ms. Marshall next door has them on her roses," I explained. "She was spraying her roses with poison. Her roses aren't far from our pizza garden and my monarch habitat. So I thought maybe if I gave her a safer spray, she might be willing to use that instead."

"Excellent idea. I think you'll need a slightly different solution for aphids, though, since you're using it as a spray instead of a dunk. Come on, let's go find one."

We went into Aunt Hannah's camper to use her computer. I don't know why Ms. Marshall doesn't like the camper. I think it's so cute, like a miniature blue house on wheels. Inside, everything is smaller than normal. It even has a tiny shower and a tiny kitchen. It's kind of like being inside a dollhouse.

We found an easy recipe online for nontoxic aphid spray made from dish soap, water, and vegetable oil. We mixed up a small batch to start with.

When we were done, Dad found an old spray bottle for me to use. I planned to take it over in the evening, when Ms. Marshall was home from work.

"Why don't I whip up a loaf of zucchini bread, as a peace offering," Dad suggested.

"Okay, but don't put anything weird in it," I warned him.

"You don't think she'd like mustard greens in her zucchini bread?"

"Dad—please, no!" Then I saw the twinkle in his eye that said he was kidding. "Da-ad!"

That afternoon, Emily and I were weeding the pizza garden and listening for Carolina wren chatter when a flash of orange caught my eye. Could it be? It was! I called Emily over. "Look—a monarch! It's found our milkweed!"

"Actually, I think it's found our pepper plants," Emily pointed out.

"Well, okay, you're right. But it's not going to lay its eggs on the pepper plants. It'll find the milkweed for that."

"It looks kind of ragged." Emily peered closer. The butterfly sat on the leaf of a pepper plant, warming its tattered black and orange wings in the sun.

"You'd look ragged, too, if you had flown two thousand miles," I told her. "Just think—it's flown through storms and wind and rain. Now it's ready to lay its eggs and start a new generation of monarchs, right here in our garden."

"You don't even know if it's a girl."
Emily has an answer for everything. I wish I did.

"Well, here goes nothing," I announced after dinner. Trying to look braver than I felt, I marched up Ms. Marshall's front walk, armed with the spray bottle in one hand and a foil-wrapped loaf of zucchini bread in the other, and rang her doorbell.

Ms. Marshall opened the door but didn't invite me in. "What can I do for you, Lanie?" she asked.

I took a deep breath. "You could stop using pesticides in your garden," I blurted out, and before she could say anything I thrust the spray bottle into her hands. "Use this instead. It's nontoxic but it will kill aphids. And if you like, I'll dig up your dandelions— that is, if you still have any. I'm good at weeding." *Stop babbling,* I told myself.

"So now *you're* telling *me* how to garden? That's an interesting twist." I couldn't tell if she was irritated or amused, but at least she didn't slam the door in my face. "Why do you care what I spray in my own garden, if I may be so bold as to ask?"

"Because our pizza garden is planted about ten

feet from your rose bed, and we eat the food we grow. In fact, my dad made this bread with some of our new zucchini." I handed her the still-warm loaf. "You should try it—it's really good. Anyway, we don't want to have poison get on it by accident, like if it's windy or something when you're spraying." I was babbling again. I always babble when I'm nervous. I decided to just stop there and not mention that I also didn't want my monarch habitat to get poison on it, seeing as how that was a bit of a sore spot with my neighbor and might turn her against the whole nontoxic spray idea.

"I see. Well. Uh, this is, uh, thoughtful of you." Ms. Marshall seemed at a loss for words. She cleared her throat. "I suppose I'm willing to give it a try. And please thank your father for the zucchini bread." She hesitated and then added, "I should tell you, though, that I've checked with the neighborhood association, and there are rules covering front yard appearance. The rules are only enforced if someone complains, and I haven't filed a complaint—yet. But I could." She paused again. "I'm trying to be fair and give you a warning."

You have to get along with your neighbors, Mom had said. I wanted to tell that to Ms. Marshall, but instead I said, "I know. I'll try to think of something soon." And

I *was* trying. But what could I do? My neighbor and I had completely different ideas on gardening and how to care for plants and growing things.

That night, I tossed and turned and couldn't sleep. Finally I gave up. I got out of bed, padded over to my desk, and switched on my computer.

From: Lanie <hollandnotthecountry@4natr.net>
To: Dakota <dakotanotthestate@4natr.net>
Date: June 30, 2010 11:32 P.M.
Subject: Life

Dakota--It's really late here, but I just can't sleep. I wish I could call you up and talk, but this is the next best thing.

I sometimes think life would be so much easier if everyone agreed on what's important. How do you explain things to people who just don't see things the way you do?

Like our next-door neighbor. She likes gardens-- as long as they're not wild and natural the way ours is. She thinks it looks messy and ugly. I wish I could find a way to make her see how cool it is.

And she's only one person. There are probably zillions of people who think this way. How can I open everyone's eyes and help them see it my way?

It was close to midnight here, but it must have been daytime in Indonesia, because I got an answer right away.

> From: Dakota <dakotanotthestate@4natr.net>
> Date: July 1, 2010 10:35 A.M.
> To: Lanie <hollandnotthecountry@4natr.net>
> Subject: Re: Life
> Hi Lanie--It's awesome to get an e-mail from you right while I'm logged on!
> I sure know what you mean about people seeing things different from how you do. I see an orangutan and think to myself, nothing's more important than helping these amazing creatures survive. But the people who cut down trees in their forest don't see the orangutan habitat--they see valuable lumber. So the trick is, how do you convince them that the orangutans are valuable, too?

I smiled. It was so comforting to talk to Dakota in real time, even though we were talking about things that made us sad. It was almost as if she was right here in the room with me instead of all the way on the other side of the planet.

I ached for her to come home.

The next day, Thursday, Nicholas came over, and I gave him a tour of our backyard. He thought my monarch habitat was cool. I was hoping we'd see more monarchs, but we only saw the same one that I'd seen yesterday. At least, it looked like the same one, but I couldn't be sure. It had moved out of the pizza garden and was sitting on a goldenrod leaf.

Factoid
Scientists tag individual monarchs by putting tiny stickers on their wings. It doesn't hurt the butterfly. That way, scientists can keep track of the butterfly.

How cool would it be if a stickered butterfly showed up in my backyard?!

Nicholas found some ladybugs on the wildflower plants, and we counted their spots. There were several two-spotters, a seven, and a twelve, but no C-9s.

"We'd better move these guys into your pizza garden," said Nicholas.

"Why?" I asked.

"Because you want monarchs to lay eggs in this part of the garden, right?"

"Well, yeah, but what does that have to do with ladybugs?" I asked.

"Ladybugs eat monarch eggs."

"WHAT?" I watched the monarch fan her orange and black wings in the morning sunlight. She'd made it all this way and now something like a cute little ladybug was going to eat her precious eggs?

"Lots of things do, Lanie. Spiders, mites, ants, lacewings, wasps, stinkbugs—"

"Are you kidding me? All those things eat monarch eggs?" I felt outraged. "The poor monarchs don't stand a chance! How are they ever going to have caterpillars?" I couldn't possibly catch every other bug in the garden just to keep it safe for monarchs.

Nicholas shrugged. "It's a cruel world out there."

I thought for a minute. In the back of my brain, I knew there had to be a simple solution to this problem. "If monarchs lay a ton of eggs while they're here, predators can't get them *all*," I said slowly. "That just means we need a ton of milkweed."

Where could I get a ton of milkweed? And the real question was, where could I plant it?

Sunday was the Fourth of July. The day dawned bright and clear. We'd had two days of heavy rain, and the air was muggy, but at least it was no longer raining. We were relieved about that, because it was Angela's turn to choose our family activity and she'd picked the Boston Pops Fireworks Spectacular, which is held outdoors.

We all got up early, because Angela wanted to be sure we got good seats in the Oval, the grassy area in front of the stage.

I poked her. "Maybe if we had camped out there the night before, we could *really* have gotten good seats!"

She laughed. "That would be my kind of camping—for front-row seats at a classical music concert!"

Mom chuckled. "Fortunately, I don't think they allow camping at the Esplanade."

Dad was planning our picnic. "We have lots of ripe cucumbers. Any votes for cucumber sandwiches?"

"I had them once," Mom replied. "I would describe them as delicately icky."

"I'll take that as a *no*, then. Maybe a chickpea salad." Dad flipped open a cookbook.

Once our meal was packed, we loaded up and drove to the river. We got wristbands that let us into the Oval. It seemed as if everyone in Boston was here.

Mom, Dad, Angela, and Emily settled onto a blanket as close to the stage as we could get, while Aunt Hannah and I wandered off between lawn chairs and blankets to check out the Charles River. A television crew passed us, lugging equipment.

That gave me an idea. I thought of Nicholas and *The Boston Globe* article about his nine-spotted ladybug discovery. What if someone interviewed me? Getting in the newspaper—or better yet, on television—would be a way to tell lots and lots of people about monarchs, and natural gardening, and how important it is to take good care of nature . . .

> *. . . There's a knock at the door. I open it. It's Ms. Marshall. "Why, Lanie," she says, "I just saw your interview on the six o'clock news, and now I understand why you planted weeds in your front yard. In fact, I've decided to dig up my roses and plant a weed garden like yours, so that I can help monarchs, too."*

I smiled. Getting interviewed couldn't be *that* hard if it had happened to Nicholas. All I had to do was discover something. Maybe I didn't have his knack for ladybugs, but I was pretty good at finding birds.

I turned to Aunt Hannah. "We need to spot
a rare bird today."

"We do?"

"Yes. It's super important." I hoped she wouldn't
ask me why, because it was sort of hard to explain.

"I'm not sure this is the best place to do that. We
might see some ducks, though. That's always fun."

Right. As if I was going to get on the news for
spotting a mallard. "Don't you always say water is a
great place for birding? Well, here we are at a big river,"
I pointed out.

"Yes, but we're also in the middle of a big city.
And with all these people here for the concert, whatever
wildlife might live in this area is making itself scarce."

Oh. So much for my big idea.

We wandered in the sticky heat until we heard
a drumroll. We hurried back to our blanket just as "The
Star-Spangled Banner" started up.

After an hour of music, the orchestra took a break.
Dad opened up our picnic basket and pulled out a plate
of surprise sandwiches—with Dad, you never know
what you might get. I had finished a cream cheese and
pimiento sandwich and was just standing up to stretch
when I felt a tap on my shoulder.

I turned and, to my astonishment, a handsome

man was saying into a microphone, "Hello, young people of Boston—what inspires *you* on this Fourth of July?" Then he looked right at me and put the microphone in my face.

Words crowded into my mind and swirled around. Usually when I'm nervous I start babbling, but suddenly I couldn't figure out how to say what I wanted to say. My brain quickly tested several possibilities: "Milkweed is very important"—no, that sounded silly. "Monarch butterflies need more habitat"—that would sound downright odd. My mind flashed on Dakota; what would she say? "People should stop logging in the orangutans' rain forest." But if I said *that*, they'd think I'd gone off the deep end.

Meanwhile, my heart was pounding, screaming to my brain, *This is your chance to reach zillions of people!! Just open your mouth and talk—now!*

I cleared my throat and tried to force a word out, any word. "Butterflies," I croaked.

Someone beside me started speaking, and the microphone shifted away from me. "I think the music is really inspiring," said a familiar voice. "I play the cello, and I'd love to play for the Boston Pops someday."

The man turned to speak into his microphone. "Well, this family has a nature lover *and* a music lover!

A Cruel World

Sounds like the Boston Pops are inspiring some real ambition in our young people today."

And before I could blink, he was gone—the man, his microphone, and his camera crew.

About an hour after the concert ended, while people were still picnicking and waiting for the fireworks to start, a thunder-and-lightning storm blew in, and Mother Nature decided to put on her own display instead. We didn't stay to watch it, though. As soon as the first fat drops started falling, we piled into the car and headed home.

In the front yard, little muddy streams were running all over the sidewalk, and our poor starter plants had been flattened in the storm. Somehow it seemed fitting, the way the whole day had just fizzled out.

I sent Dakota an e-mail before going to sleep.

From: Lanie <hollandnotthecountry@4natr.net>
To: Dakota <dakotanotthestate@4natr.net>
Date: July 4, 2010 11:05 P.M.
Subject: I give up

Lately I can't seem to do anything right. Maybe I should forget about making a Monarch Waystation and just concentrate on becoming a scientist, like my aunt. She gets to visit cool places like Hawaii and Costa Rica to record birdcalls, and then she listens to the recordings and writes about them on her computer. You'll love Aunt Hannah when you meet her.

Anyway, I just wanted to tell you that things aren't going too well here. All I've seen is one raggedy monarch, and it's already July.

I miss you so much. When are you coming home?

Monday morning I woke to a bright, sunny day, and for a split second I felt cheerful and happy—until I remembered: I'd been given a once-in-a-lifetime chance and I'd blown it. I'd never have another chance like that to speak out and tell people about important things like monarchs and orangutans and taking care of nature. Even though the sunlight was streaming in my window, I felt as if I had a dark, heavy cloud inside my heart.

After breakfast, Emily wanted to take Lulu for a walk in the backyard. I put on Lulu's harness and leash and set her in the bunny elevator. Mom had built a dumbwaiter in the middle of our open staircase so that we wouldn't have to carry laundry up and down two flights of stairs, but I like to use it for Lulu. Emily waited downstairs and took Lulu out of the elevator and onto the kitchen deck. Lulu gave a leap and a wiggle in midair— a joyful bunny dance to say, *I'm so happy to be outside!*

"Can you check the wren's nest?" Emily asked

Aunt Hannah, who was sitting on a deck chair with a cup of coffee.

"Honey, I think the wrens found another home," Aunt Hannah said gently. "I've checked it every day, and it's still empty."

"Can't you check again?" Emily begged.

"Tell you what—let's look around the yard and listen. Maybe we'll see some other birds."

Emily looked disappointed, but she let Lulu lead her around the yard, with Aunt Hannah and me following.

I hadn't been in the yard for several days because of all the rain, and it was amazing how much things had changed in a short time. In the pizza garden, the cherry tomatoes were already turning red, the oregano was sprouting tiny pinkish-purple flowers, and the basil was bursting with new leaves in various shades of green and purple. We had planted chocolate basil and pineapple basil along with the regular Italian kind. I picked a few leaves and pinched them, comparing the pungent aromas.

"Nothing like a few days of rain to give everything a shot of new growth," Aunt Hannah remarked.

In the monarch habitat, the plants looked as if they'd grown ten inches in the last four days. They were bushy and full instead of spindly and straggly, and the bare ground was no longer visible between the plants. The garden didn't look as much like a weed patch anymore. On several plants, large flower buds had formed. I was eager to see what they would look like when they opened . . .

. . . Bright orange and black butterflies flutter from blossom to blossom, sipping nectar. The plants are a dazzling rainbow of color, all blooming at once. Even the milkweeds are covered with puffy purple flowers. Ms. Marshall gazes at the sight, her jaw dropping open at the sheer beauty. "You were right, Lanie," she says. "These are the most beautiful flowers I've ever seen."

"Lanie! Hello there, Lanie?"

Aunt Hannah nudged me. "Your neighbor is calling you. You'd better go see what she wants."

Startled, I looked up. Standing by her rosebushes, Ms. Marshall waved and beckoned me over.

The rain had given the roses a growth spurt, too. Their glossy leaves shone bright green in the sunlight, and the flower buds had opened into perfect roses of pearly white and soft shades of peach and pink. A delicate scent perfumed the air. It smelled sort of like my favorite shampoo, and I was about to ask my neighbor if she used the same kind I did, when I realized that it was the roses I was smelling.

"Nice morning, isn't it," she said pleasantly.

I nodded, wary.

"The roses have started blooming. I thought you might like to see them." She hesitated. "I know you like gardens."

I nodded again. *Say something.* "I see them. They're—they're awesome." I didn't want to admit it, but I had to be honest about it.

She smiled, and it was a real smile, not a stiff one. But the smile faded as she reached for a leaf—not a glossy, diamond-shaped leaf but a dull, raggedy, curled-up leaf. "Oh no." She turned the leaf over and uncurled it to reveal a cluster of tiny gray-green bumps. I caught my breath. Suddenly I understood exactly how she felt, because I felt it, too: how dare those aphids attack these beautiful plants!

"Did you try the soap spray?" I asked.

Ms. Marshall nodded. "Yes. It seemed to kill the aphids, but I think it doesn't keep on working days later, the way the commercial sprays do. It must have washed off in the rain. So now I have aphids again."

"Would you like me to spray them for you? I could inspect your roses every day and spray whenever I find aphids."

"That's a nice offer, Lanie. But that's quite a job. Do you really want to take that on? I know you're very busy with your own garden." If she was thinking, *and the new front lawn you're going to be planting*, at least she didn't say it. Yet, anyway.

"Sure, I can do that," I told her. "I'm out here almost every day anyway. I wouldn't mind."

"Well, okay then. I'll go get the soap spray right now. I have to run some errands—will you be all right on your own here?"

I nodded. Just then I heard Emily calling. She was coming around the side of our garden shed with Lulu, and she sounded excited.

"Lanie, Aunt Hannah, come over here! Bring the ladder!"

A male Carolina wren was perched on the roof of the garden shed, just as we'd seen him the other day, and as we came near he started to scold loudly. Under the eave of the shed, we could hear the buzzing chatter of the female. The noise was coming from inside an old watering can that was hanging just under the eave at the back of the shed.

"That's where she's put her new nest—right in that watering can!" said Aunt Hannah. "We won't bother the wrens now, but once they get used to us coming near them, we can climb up and peek inside to get a look at the eggs."

Those wrens had been crafty in finding a safe spot for their nest. It would be impossible for a cat to reach it. And when the baby wrens hatched, we would get to watch them grow.

Ms. Marshall returned with the sprayer, and I got to work. She had a lot of rosebushes—thirty-six in all, counting the ones in the front yard. I tried to be thorough. It took a lot longer than I expected, as I ran out of spray and had to mix another batch before I was done. Then I searched her lawn for weeds and pulled out anything that didn't look like grass, just to be sure she wouldn't use her herbicide spray. The whole job took several hours. It was past noon by the time I finished, and I was exhausted. I wondered if I could manage to do this job every single day.

After showering and eating lunch, I checked my computer. Dakota had sent a reply to last night's e-mail.

From: Dakota <dakotanotthestate@4natr.net>
Date: July 5, 2010 10:08 A.M.
To: Lanie <hollandnotthecountry@4natr.net>
Subject: Re: I give up
   Dear Lanie, please don't give up. If people like you--people who really care--just give up, then who will save the plants and animals and wild places that need our help?

That one was easy:

From: "Lanie" <hollandnotthecountry@4natr.net>
To: "Dakota" <dakotanotthestate@4natr.net>
Date: July 5, 2010 1:32 P.M.
Subject: Re: I give up
   Grown-ups will take care of them. People like my Aunt Hannah and our fourth-grade teacher, Mr. James. They're smart and they know how to do stuff. I'm just one kid. It was dumb to think that I could do something important and make a difference in the world.

I shut off my computer, fed Lulu, and settled down on my bed to make some field notes in my journal. I described the wren nest in the watering can and drew a little sketch. Then I fell asleep.

After a long nap, I awoke feeling sort of dazed. I wandered downstairs to the living room, where Angela and some of her music friends were practicing. She and two friends had formed a trio, which means three people playing together, and they were doing songs for violin, viola, and cello. It sounded really pretty, much better than one cello by itself. I slid open the deck door and lay in the hammock and just listened, remembering our camping trip and how magical the music had sounded outside under the trees.

That night, my long nap made it hard for me to fall asleep. I couldn't stop thinking about Ms. Marshall—how her roses were being attacked by aphids—and about our torn-up front yard and how ugly it was to her. I hated the idea that my yard was making her unhappy just as much as I hated the idea of her organizing the neighbors against us. Still, I had to face the fact that taking care of her yard as well as mine was too much for me. But if I couldn't convince her to garden without poison spray, then what was I doing inviting monarchs into *my* yard? Every time an innocent butterfly landed on a rosebush, it would die.

I thought of the ragged little monarch that had come to my garden. Out of the whole country, it had chosen *my* yard. Didn't I owe it a safe place to stay and lay its eggs?

Don't give up—that was easy for Dakota to say. She didn't know how impossible my problem was.

Since I was awake anyway, I got up and checked my e-mail again.

> From: Dakota <dakotanotthestate@4natr.net>
> Date: July 6, 2010 10:04 A.M.
> To: Lanie <hollandnotthecountry@4natr.net>
> Subject: Re: I give up
>
> Lanie, it was not dumb to think you could make a difference--YOU CAN. Just because everything isn't going perfectly doesn't mean you should give up. Just think: if everyone did that, nothing would get accomplished.
>
> And besides, who do you think will be the

grown-ups in a few years? U & me! So why wait? There are important things that need doing right now!

I glanced at the clock. Once again, it was nearly midnight—which meant it was nearly midday in Indonesia. I typed a reply, hoping that Dakota might be logged on.

From: Lanie <hollandnotthecountry@4natr.net>
To: Dakota <dakotanotthestate@4natr.net>
Date: July 5, 2010 11:15 P.M.
Subject: Re: I give up
   I know what you're saying, but it all just feels so hopeless. I mean, even if I stop my neighbor from using pesticides in her garden, there are zillions of other people who will still use them. I can't stop them all.

I waited a few minutes—and sure enough, my computer pinged with a reply!

From: Dakota <dakotanotthestate@4natr.net>
Date: July 6, 2010 10:19 A.M.
To: Lanie <hollandnotthecountry@4natr.net>
Subject: Re: I give up

It might seem that way, but that's exactly why you shouldn't give up! Remember, change happens one person at a time.

In the villages around here, many of the men used to work as loggers. Now that this area is a protected park, some of them work as guides, leading tours of the orangutan forest. This way they can earn a living without hurting the orangutans' habitat. Unfortunately, the wood is so valuable that there's still a lot of illegal logging going on.

It takes money to spread the word and help people learn new ways of doing things. The orangutan conservation center doesn't have enough money for this. So my parents are helping raise money--that's why we stayed longer than we had planned.

But guess what--we'll be home in 10 days! Eeee!

As I read Dakota's e-mail, my emotions zigzagged like a pinball. First, sadness and worry about the orangutans —and then a wild bounce of joy: at last, Dakota was coming home!

Tuesday I had my class again at the community gardens. The roses would have to wait. I hoped that the thorough spraying I had given them yesterday would last through today, since it hadn't rained.

Aunt Hannah had to go to the university and couldn't take me to the community gardens, so I rode my bike. When I got there, Nicholas was waiting for me.

"Hey, Lanie, check out all the monarchs!" he said as soon as I had parked my bike.

They were everywhere, fluttering gracefully among the vegetable plants and even in the weed patch that ran along the far edge of the gardens. A few butterflies looked a bit tattered, like the one in my yard, but most of them looked strong and healthy, with crisp, perfectly formed orange-and-black-patterned wings.

"Wow, I wonder why there are so many of them here," I marveled. "I wish a few of them would come to *my* garden."

"Well, they're probably just starting to discover your garden, since it's a new place for them," Nicholas suggested.

A new place for them . . . But how could I make sure it was a *safe* place?

Mr. James greeted us. "Nice to see you again, boys

and girls. What a great day for gardening! The cucumbers and sugar snap peas are ripe, and after all this rain, the weeds are sliding out like a knife through butter. We'll weed for an hour, take a break, and then harvest the cukes and peas. Grab your tools and find a spot."

Nicholas and I settled in to weed the carrot patch and watch for ladybugs. In the past I had always thought ladybugs were cute, but with all the monarchs around, I didn't feel so thrilled to see them.

"Nicholas, why do people say ladybugs are good for the garden, if they eat monarch eggs?"

"Well, that's not all they eat."

"It's not?" I stood up to yank on a tall weed. The vegetables weren't the only plants that had grown in the past week—the rain had given the weeds a burst of growth, too.

"No. They eat garden pests as well."

"Like what?"

"Mites. Mealybugs. Aphids."

"Aphids?" The weed's long taproot suddenly slid out of the soil, and I fell backward onto my butt. "Ladybugs eat aphids?"

"Yup." I could tell Nicholas was trying not to laugh at my fall.

But I didn't care. Suddenly, I loved ladybugs.

At the break, I asked Mr. James if he had a container with a lid. He gave me an empty plastic food tub that he had brought for collecting peas. I punched holes in the lid to make a temporary ladybug home.

I told Nicholas all about my next-door neighbor, her roses, and the aphids. "So we have to catch zillions of ladybugs. Then I'll release them on her roses, and they'll eat the aphids, and nobody will have to spray them."

Nicholas nodded. "Farmers do that, you know."

"Do what? Catch ladybugs?"

"No, use them for pest control. They buy huge batches of ladybugs by mail order and release them in their fields."

Was there anything Nicholas didn't know about ladybugs?

We worked our way to the back of the garden and decided to try the weedy strip on the far side of the path. It was harder going—some of the weeds were almost waist-high—but there were lots of ladybugs. Even I was striking it rich.

As I popped another red beetle into the container, I felt a warm wave of gratitude toward Nicholas. "Did you know that humans have about nine thousand taste buds on their tongues, but rabbits have about seventeen thousand?" I asked him.

"Seriously? I did not know that." He paused, thinking, then lobbed me one. "Did you know that Indonesia has fish that climb trees to catch insects?"

"Really? Hey, my best friend has been living in Indonesia! I'll have to ask her if she's seen any tree-climbing fish." I told him all about Dakota and the orangutan conservation center. "Did you know that ninety-seven percent of orangutans' genes are just the same as ours? That makes them one of our closest relatives in the animal world." I wondered if people with indoor genes might be only ninety-five or ninety six percent the same as orangutans, but I didn't say anything about that to Nicholas.

We moved to another weed patch. Whoa—this plant looked familiar.

"Hey, Nicholas, check it out—there's a ton of milkweed here." I scanned the area. The pale, big-leafed plants were all over the place, hundreds of them. Maybe even thousands. No wonder there were so many monarchs around.

I started examining all the weeds more closely. Some were just thistles and dandelions, plants we were pulling out of the vegetable garden, but others looked awfully similar to things growing in my backyard—except the ones here were already starting to bloom.

The bee balm, which I knew by its sparse, jagged-edged leaves and minty smell, had purplish tufts at the top of each tall stalk. The black-eyed Susans had golden-yellow, daisy-like petals around black centers, and the Queen Anne's lace had feathery leaves and flat clusters of tiny white flowers at the top that really looked like lace. And all around, bright orange monarchs were everywhere, flitting from blossom to blossom. They looked happy.

In fact, everything here looked happy, including the people. I gazed down the long row of community gardens, where kids and families were working together, and into the park and ball fields beyond, where more people were gathered, and suddenly I had an idea.

"Ready to pick peas?" Mr. James asked, calling us back to the vegetable garden. He handed us each a plastic milk jug with its top cut off and a string running through the handle. "If you tie the string around your waist, you can keep your hands free while you pick." He showed us how to identify peas that were ripe and ready for picking.

We picked peas for a while and then moved on to cucumbers, which were surprisingly tricky for such big vegetables. You'd think you had picked every cuke on a vine, and then suddenly see one you'd totally missed, lying there like a humongous pickle.

Finally we were done, and Mr. James collected our harvest. "Wow, that's a lot of peas and cucumbers. Would anyone like to take some home?"

I already had my ladybugs to take home, and since I was riding my bike, I couldn't carry anything more. But before I left, I had a question.

"Mr. James, do you think we could have a garden festival here? There's so much cool stuff to see and do. My little sister is dying to come out here, and I know she would love picking peas. You could give a class in organic gardening. I could give tours of the wildflowers over there"—I pointed to the weed strip—"and Nicholas could show kids how to catch ladybugs and count their spots. Maybe we'll even find a C-9! That's a nine-spotted ladybug—they're very rare. Nicholas found one once and got in the newspaper." I realized I was babbling, but this time I wasn't nervous, just excited. "Anyway, what do you think?"

Here's what *I* was thinking: a garden festival might not pull in as many people as the Boston Pops, but it would still be a chance to do what Dakota had said— to spread the word and show new ways of doing things.

"I think that's a great idea, Lanie," said Mr. James. "Why don't you talk to your parents about it, and if they approve, I'll be glad to help you organize it."

At dinner that night, I shared my idea for a garden festival with my family. To my surprise, despite their indoor genes, they liked the idea—and even wanted to help.

"I could play birdsongs and show people how to recognize the birds in this area," Aunt Hannah offered.

"I could build a garden shed out of recycled building materials, to show how easily old building materials can be reused instead of thrown away," Mom added.

"And I could sell things," said Dad.

I raised my eyebrows. "What kinds of things were you thinking of selling?"

"Things from the garden, of course," he said. "Little bunches of herbs. Jars of my famous tomato-jalapeno jelly."

"You'll have to give people free tastes of that before they buy—that's only fair," said Angela, and we all laughed.

"If we sell things, what would the money be used for?" Mom asked.

I hadn't thought about that; I had just been imagining a free festival. But now that my parents had brought it up, I liked the idea of selling stuff. Because

I knew exactly what the money could be used for.

"To help orangutans," I said, and filled them in on everything Dakota had told me.

After dinner, I picked up my ladybugs and headed out the front door. I tried not to look at our bedraggled front yard, so that I wouldn't spoil my happy mood. The wildflower seeds Aunt Hannah and I had planted hadn't come up yet, or maybe they had gotten washed away in the Fourth of July storm. And the starter plants still looked half-dead, although a few were showing a tiny bit of new growth at the tips.

Ms. Marshall answered my knock right away. "Hello, Lanie. Have you come to check on the roses? I just got home from work and haven't looked at them yet. Would you like to join me now?" I saw her glance at our front yard, but she didn't say anything about it, so I pretended not to notice.

"Sure," I said. We walked through her house and out onto her back terrace. "Here —I brought you something." I handed her the container.

Her eyes widened and she gave a little gasp as she realized the inside was crawling with ladybugs, but she kept her cool and didn't drop the container.

"For the roses," I quickly explained. "Ladybugs love to eat aphids. It's one of their favorite foods." I felt like a ladybug salesman. "Did you know that farmers even buy ladybugs through the mail and put them on their fields to control aphids and other bugs that hurt their crops?"

"Really?" Ms. Marshall shook her head. "That's interesting, Lanie. I thought farmers used chemical pesticides."

"Well, some do, but not all of them. Using ladybugs is a lot safer, especially around food crops."

"Like your vegetable garden."

"Yes. And—" I figured I might as well say it, "and also around food for butterflies, like my monarch habitat." I hesitated and then added, "Pesticides kill butterflies," just to be sure she got the point.

"I see." She stopped in front of the first rosebush and held out the container to me. "Well, here we are. Would you like to do the honors?"

I opened the lid and sprinkled the ladybugs around the roses, trying to get a few on each bush, but she had so many rosebushes, I ran out of ladybugs way before I had done all the bushes. "I'll get some more ladybugs tomorrow," I promised.

"Where are you getting them, if I may ask?"

I told her about the community gardens. Then I told her about the festival. "It's a week from Saturday. Can you come?"

"I'll have to check my calendar. But thank you for the invitation."

"You're welcome. Well, I guess I'd better go." It was getting dark.

"Lanie?" She cleared her throat. "Any thoughts on your front yard?"

I shrugged. "Not really."

She nodded. "Well, good night."

I knew I couldn't put it off forever. But suddenly, the front yard didn't seem so important anymore. After all, the monarchs had plenty of milkweed at the community gardens, far more than I could ever give them.

For the next week, it seemed as if all anyone talked about was the festival. At home, Mom showed me her design for a garden shed made out of old doors and windows of various shapes. It was quirky but charming, with the doors in different colors and cute flower boxes sized to the different windows. Dad started whipping up batches of jelly and salsa and experimenting with new recipes, trying them out on us at dinner. And when I asked Angela and her friends if their trio could play music at the festival, I could tell she was pleased and flattered, even though she tried to act cool about it.

I talked to Nicholas and Mr. James almost every day, either at the community gardens or by phone, making plans. Mr. James had recruited other parents to contribute activities and things to sell, and Nicholas was planning to hold a ladybug-catching contest at the festival.

I brought Emily to the community gardens to catch ladybugs with Nicholas and me a few times. Other than butterflies, Emily has never liked bugs because they're so crawly, but she thinks ladybugs are cute, and she turned out to be excellent at catching them, with her sharp eyes and small fingers. Whenever our talk turned to the festival, though, she pouted.

"What can *I* do for the garden festival? You guys are leaving me out."

"There will be lots of things you can help with, Emily," I told her. "You could sell lemonade—"

"I don't want to *help*, I want to *do* something. And not sell lemonade—that's Dad's thing."

Making Plans

I understood how she felt. Food was *Dad's* specialty. Emily wanted to make a more personal contribution, just as the rest of us were doing. "We'll figure out something special for you to do," I told her, although I had no idea what.

I e-mailed Dakota all about the festival. She was thrilled at the idea of raising money for the orangutans—and even more thrilled that she would be home in time to help out. The only person even more thrilled than she was about that was me.

I couldn't wait to show Dakota our backyard. Since she had left, seven long months ago, our yard had been totally transformed. The pizza garden was bursting with peppers and tomatoes and fragrant herbs, and the wildflowers in the monarch garden had finally started blooming. It wasn't exactly the dazzling rainbow garden of my fantasy, but the shy, delicate wild blossoms seemed even more special, somehow. Every day more and more flowers opened, and Emily, Aunt Hannah, and I liked trying to spot the new ones. Best of all, the monarchs liked them. So far, we had counted five butterflies that had moved in!

In the watering can under the garden-shed roof, our Carolina wrens had laid four tiny, pale pink eggs with rust-brown flecks. Aunt Hannah said they would hatch in about two weeks, but Emily couldn't wait. She made Aunt Hannah set up the ladder every day, just to check.

Now if my monarchs would just lay some eggs, I thought to myself, it really would be Monarch Heaven.

When the daily e-mails stopped, I knew that meant Dakota was finally on her way home. The whole day I could barely eat or sleep. The next morning at breakfast, I kept running to the window every time I heard a car go by, to see if anyone was pulling up in front of our house.

"Chill out, Lanie," Angela told me. "I'm sure she'll call before she comes over."

"But what if she's already home?"

"She might need a nap first," Mom pointed out. "It's about a thirty-six-hour trip. She'll be pretty jet-lagged."

I was feeling a bit jet-lagged myself, what with not sleeping soundly the previous night. Whenever I had awakened, I had checked my e-mail, just to make sure there was nothing from Dakota. For the first time, I was hoping there wouldn't be—and there wasn't. I was going to see her soon!

At last the phone call came. We were squealing and laughing so much, we could barely talk. It was so good to hear her voice.

Dakota's mom drove her over after lunch. We hugged and jumped up and down, and then she hugged everyone in my family while her mom hugged me. Then Dakota reached into a bag and pulled out the cutest stuffed animal I had ever seen. It had big, melting brown eyes and long, soft orange fur—my very own baby orangutan.

"Remember baby Fio? This one looks just like her," Dakota said. "She wasn't much bigger than that when she arrived at the center."

I hugged the orangutan. "Oh, I just love her. I'm going to call her Fio. Thank you!" I hugged Dakota again, too.

"You're welcome," said Dakota. "By the way, what happened to your front lawn?" she asked, when we were done hugging.

"Well, it was supposed to be more monarch habitat, but I think we planted it too late." I took her arm. "Come and see the backyard instead."

After a tour of the backyard, Mom drove us all over to the community gardens. Dad and Aunt Hannah were at the university, but Emily and Angela came along. The festival was tomorrow, and we wanted to see how all the preparations were coming. Mom was putting the finishing touches on her booth, and Angela wanted to check out the park shelter where the musicians would be playing.

Stop!

"Did you bring the ladybug carrier?" Emily asked.

I held up the plastic tub. "Right here."

"Why do you need a ladybug carrier?" Dakota asked.

"So we can *carry* them. Duh!" Emily gave Dakota a superior look.

Dakota and I exchanged a smile over Emily's head. Then I told her all about my anti-aphid campaign, and she immediately signed on as a ladybug wrangler.

The community gardens were a buzzing hive of activity. In the parking lot, people were taking folding chairs and tables out of several vans and carrying them to the park shelter. Others were putting out large garbage cans. Some men were setting up portable toilets. A man on a loud riding lawnmower was mowing the grass that surrounded the garden area, and in the gardens, people were busy picking veggies, hoeing weeds, spreading wood chips on the paths, and generally spiffing things up for the festival.

I left Mom and Angela at the booth and headed to the weed-and-wildflower strip with Emily and Dakota. As we dodged around the tractor mower and waded into the tall weeds, I heard Dakota catch her breath at all the monarchs, their orange wings flashing in the sunlight.

I could have kissed her. Here was a girl who had just spent seven months living with orangutans—one of the all-time amazing animals of the world—and she could still be thrilled by monarchs.

I pointed out milkweed and several of the key nectar-producing flowers, while Emily told Dakota how monarch caterpillars eat nothing but milkweed until they form pupas. Once they hatch out into butterflies, they live on nectar while they find milkweed to lay their eggs on, and the cycle begins again.

"How long do they live?" Dakota asked.

I knew the answer to that, because it was so fascinating. "Every summer, the first three generations of monarchs each live and die over a period of about eight weeks. But the fourth generation is special and lives much longer. Those butterflies migrate south for the winter, and they return the following summer to lay their eggs."

"What do the eggs look like?" asked Emily.

"They're tiny and white, about the size of a pin-head. I've only seen them in pictures." The drone of the tractor was getting louder, and I had to sort of shout to be heard. "You're supposed to look for them on the underside of milkweed leaves, but I haven't found any yet," I shouted.

Stop!

"Like this?" Emily shouted back. She was kneeling down and peering under a milkweed leaf. I squatted next to her and flipped over the leaf. A tiny white egg stuck out from the leaf, as if it was glued on at one end. It looked exactly like the pictures I'd seen on the Monarch Watch Web site. But this was the real thing.

I hugged my sister. "Emily, you're not only the champion ladybug finder, you're the first one to find a monarch egg!" Nicholas and I had been keeping an eye out for them ever since the monarchs had arrived two weeks ago, but we hadn't had any luck. "You should be an entomologist, Emily. That's a bug scientist."

Emily looked up at me, her eyes shining. This was the same little sister who just a few months ago couldn't stand to be anywhere near a bug—and now she was positively glowing because she had discovered a butter-fly egg. And why not? It was a thrilling discovery.

"That little thing will turn into a Stripey?" Emily asked.

"Yup." Stripey was a monarch caterpillar that had been in Emily's classroom last year. In fact, Stripey was what first got my sister and me interested in mon-archs. When I thought about it, I owed a lot to Stripey.

"Lanie—look out!" screamed Dakota.

I spun around. For one chaotic moment, I couldn't

tell what was happening. The air was swirling with bits of plants and dirt and noise. Then I saw the riding mower heading straight into our weed patch.

I didn't have time to think. I didn't have time to be scared. I didn't have time to stop myself. I hurtled desperately toward the mower, waving my arms and screaming, "No! Stop!"

The roaring engine died. "What are you girls doing in here?" called the teenage boy driving the mower. "Get out of the way!"

"I think the real question is, what are *you* doing in here?" I shot back.

He raised his hands. "We're getting this area cleaned up so it'll look nice for the festival."

Cleaned up? Look NICE? my brain screamed back at him. I had never been so angry in my life. He had no idea what he was doing—he didn't even know he was destroying milkweed and murdering monarchs! Furious words crowded into my mind and started swirling around like the chopped-up weeds in the mower. Then I felt Dakota's hand on my arm, and she gave it a squeeze. I took a deep breath and let it out slowly.

"Actually, this area is perfect just the way it is," I told him calmly. "It's full of important plants that are needed by the monarch butterfly."

"It's a monarch nursery," Dakota chimed in. "We're studying it and collecting specimens."

"Wanna see a monarch egg?" Emily asked.

"Nah, that's okay. Lemme just turn this thing around, and I'll stay out of your way." He reached for the ignition.

"Don't mow *any weeds* in this area!" I shouted as the engine roared to life.

He nodded and gave me a thumbs-up.

I could hardly believe it. Just by opening my mouth and saying *stop*, I had saved a whole field of milkweed—and a whole generation of monarchs.

Who knew that protecting wildlife could sometimes be that simple?

The morning of the festival dawned bright and clear. We hurried through breakfast, and then Mom, Dad, Emily, and I started packing up the car. Aunt Hannah was driving her camper with Angela and the cello. As we were finishing loading up, I saw Ms. Marshall in her front yard with a pair of pruners, snipping her rosebushes.

"Hi, Ms. Marshall," I said. "How are the roses doing?"

"Aphid-free, so far," she said with a smile. "They're all done blooming, so I'm just trimming off the old wilted blossoms to keep them looking neat and tidy." She snipped a branch. "Here's a question for *you*, Lanie—"

"I know what you're going to ask," I said. "It's about the front yard. Right?"

She raised her eyebrows but didn't say anything.

"I—I've decided to take these plants out," I announced. I didn't know that I had decided this until that very moment, but maybe my brain had decided it earlier and just not told me, because I instantly knew it was the right decision. "I'm sorry the front yard has been looking so awful," I added. Most of the starter plants had died; the few that still showed signs of life I would transplant into the backyard to join the monarch habitat. I didn't know what I would replace them with, though. Something other than a lawn, I hoped, so Dad wouldn't have to mow it.

"I'm sorry your plants didn't do well," said Ms. Marshall. "I know how discouraging that can be." Then she gave me a smile, a friendly one. "But I've been meaning to tell you how lovely your wildflower garden looks now, with everything in bloom. I've been enjoying it when I'm in my backyard."

"You have? Really? That's awesome!" I beamed at her. "Are you coming to the garden festival today?"

"I'm hoping to make it later on," she said brightly, but I couldn't tell if she really meant it or was just being polite.

We drove off in a car-and-camper caravan. At the festival site, I gazed slowly around the park and community gardens, awed at the transformation. Mom's garden shed looked like a little house from a nursery rhyme, with mismatched doors and shutters in various colors, and potted plants blooming in the window boxes. Dad unloaded boxes of jars and herbs from the car and began arranging them on tables. Aunt Hannah helped Angela carry her cello to the park shelter, and soon the husky sound of the cello was joined by the silvery sound of violin strings as the musicians began tuning up.

Dakota and her mom arrived, carrying two huge signs that read, "Save the Rain Forest for the Orangutans!" They put the signs on a table near the garden shed, where they could talk to people, hand out flyers, and take donations.

I brought Fio over and set her on the table next to one of the signs. She looked so adorable—I hoped she would attract lots of people to their table.

Nicholas and Emily had made signs announcing a ladybug-catching contest and a tour of the monarch nursery. Soon more and more people started arriving, and the festival was on.

I kept watching for Ms. Marshall, hoping she would show up. I wanted to introduce her to Nicholas, ladybug expert extraordinaire. At last I spotted her at the far end of the gardens, near the park shelter where Angela and her trio were playing. I hurried over.

"Ms. Marshall—you came!"

She gave me a smile and a nod, and then she put her finger to her lips and pointed at the musicians. We stood and listened for a few minutes as the music floated out on the warm summer air.

When the song ended, I pointed to Angela. "That's my sister, on the cello."

Ms. Marshall's eyes widened. "Really? Why, she's very talented. You know, I do marketing for the Boston Pops. Has she ever considered a career in classical music? If she wanted to play in a youth chamber group, I could probably arrange an audition."

I nodded solemnly. "She would love that, I'm sure."

"You'll have to introduce us later, when she's done playing." Ms. Marshall turned to me. "Shall we go and shop some of the flower booths? I hear the festival is raising money for a worthy cause."

Ms. Marshall and I strolled past the tables, oohing and ahhing at all the flowers. Suddenly we both stopped at a table that was overflowing with blossoms—brilliant bursts of pink, red, orange, and yellow. On the ground, one pot held ferny plants, one was filled with hot magenta daisies, and another had tall delicate flower spikes of electric blue. The scene vaguely reminded me of something, but I couldn't think where I had seen such flowers before. They weren't anything I recognized, that was for sure.

"How beautiful," Ms. Marshall breathed. "Your flowers are positively breathtaking."

"What kinds of flowers are these?" I asked the lady

who was selling them.

"Oh, it's a little of everything," she said. "On the table we have dahlias, nasturtiums, and zinnias." She gestured at the magenta daisies and tall blue spikes. "These are cosmos and larkspur. Mostly annuals, but a lot of them will reseed themselves. They make great aphid decoys."

My ears perked up. "Great what?" Suddenly I flashed on my rainbow flower fantasy. That was why these flowers seemed vaguely familiar.

"Decoys. Aphids love them, prefer them actually. It's a proven method of natural pest control. Aphids'll come to these plants and leave your ornamentals alone."

My neighbor and I looked at each other, and I knew we were thinking the same thing. In that moment, I knew exactly what I was going to plant in the front yard.

Someone tapped me on the shoulder, and I turned to see Mr. James and a very tall man holding a notebook.

"Lanie, this Mark, from *The Boston Globe*. He's doing a story on the festival," said Mr. James. "I told him it was all your idea, so he wants to interview you. Your parents said it was okay with them if it's okay with you."

The Boston Globe? I nodded, willing my brain to

not freeze up. Then Mark started asking questions like how I got the idea for the festival and why we were raising money for orangutans, which I had no trouble answering. I didn't even babble or get brain freeze.

"Last question, Lanie: What's the one thing you want my readers to know?" Mark asked.

I thought about what to say. *Don't use pesticides? Save the rain forest? Recycle?* They were all important. How could I pick just one thing?

Ms. Marshall was still standing by the flower table, listening to my interview. When I glanced at her, she smiled encouragingly and nodded, as if she agreed with everything I had said so far.

I looked around at the festival and thought to myself, *I did this.* A troupe of kids were out in the weed patch hunting for ladybugs with Nicholas and Emily. Aunt Hannah was teaching some people to identify different birdcalls. Mom was showing off her recycled garden shed to a bunch of admiring ladies, and Dad was already sold out of salsa. At the orangutan table, Dakota was talking earnestly to a group of adults. Looking up, she caught my eye, grinned, and gave me a thumbs-up.

I turned to the *Globe* reporter. "Don't give up."

Mark squinted as if he didn't quite understand. "Excuse me?"

The Garden Festival

Dakota was right—why wait for grown-ups to figure everything out? "There are lots of things each of us, even kids, can do every day to help the earth," I explained. "The plants and animals are depending on us. So the important thing is to *do* it and don't give up!"

Letter from American Girl

Dear Readers,

Every girl can make a difference when it comes to protecting the earth. Here are the stories of four real girls who are passionate about the environment and who—with the help of their families, friends, and classmates—are working hard to protect it. Like Lanie's friend Nicholas, one girl and her brother found a rare ladybug. Another girl has found her favorite spot on earth and does everything she can to take care of it, much as Lanie does. Another has learned all about an endangered species and the challenges it faces, just as Dakota does. Finally, like many of you who write to us, one girl is helping preserve resources through recycling. We hope you are inspired by these real girls and their real stories.

There are many ways to help; the important thing is to find your passion and get started!

Your friends at American Girl

LOVING LADYBUGS

When 11-year-old insect hunter Jilene P. and her 10-year-old brother, Jonathan, discovered a nine-spotted ladybug near their Virginia home, it was a rare find. In fact, it was the first sighting of this native ladybug in the eastern United States in more than 14 years.

The nine-spotted ladybug—called a C-9—eats many species of aphids and other crop pests and can live in many different crops. This has made C-9s valuable to farmers and foresters, who have long used them for natural pest control. But there have been fewer and fewer C-9 sightings since the 1990s. No one knows for sure why they are now so rare. Their disappearance may be due to a combination of habitat loss and invasion by other types of ladybugs and beetles. But researchers want to find out!

Jilene and Jonathan started collecting insects to help a friend, Jordan, who was majoring in entomology—the study of insects—in college. They sent her everything they collected, and when Jordan and her professor saw the rare C-9, they started the Lost Ladybug Project as a database to keep track of the C-9 and other native ladybug species.

Among other valuable information, the Virginia sighting proved that the species is not extinct—and that there may be hope for a C-9 revival.

Jilene is always on the lookout for another C-9. "I loved learning about the ladybug life cycle," says Jilene, who developed a presentation about it that earned her a Bronze Award in Girl Scouts. "It's important to remember that when we talk about the environment, we have to include even the smallest creatures—even insects!"

The Lost Ladybug Project—and Other Web Sites

For information about the Lost Ladybug Project, go to www.lostladybug.org. Help keep track of fireflies at www.mos.org/fireflywatch/. Help scientists keep track of monarchs at www.monarchwatch.org/.

IN THE WOODS

Sabra M. has really tall neighbors—more than 250 feet tall, to be exact. That's because this California girl lives near thick forests of redwood trees, the tallest plants in the world.

Sabra, 12, loves the redwoods and the forest creatures so much that she works as a junior ranger, going into the forest almost every day in the summertime. "We learn about the animals and their habitats, geology, and the environment of the redwoods," explains the outdoor adventurer, who counts an endangered bird called the marbled murrelet as her favorite forest dweller.

Junior rangers help pick up trash around campsites, go on nature hikes, and learn the park rules, such as staying on the trails. "If you don't stay on the trails, you can cause erosion and ruin the animals' habitats," warns Sabra. "We need to learn to care for the earth."

At night, junior rangers help put on educational programs for campers. Sabra is passionate about teaching others to respect the great outdoors. "It's important to me to help so that parks are preserved for many generations to come."

PAPER RECYCLER

Most girls don't like to think about garbage. But trash was all that Julia U. had on her mind after her science class studied natural resources and she learned how many trees are destroyed to make paper.

"I realized our school had no recycling bins," says the 9-year-old Maryland girl. "If we don't recycle, more trees get cut down, which means more animals need to find new shelter."

Julia turned to the student council for help. She gave a speech to the council about how bins could help the earth.

The student council formed a recycling committee and got to work, with Julia's help. "I did online research about what companies offer bins," she remembers. Finally, Julia heard that the bins had been ordered.

Months went by, and no bins arrived. But when Julia walked down the hall on the first day of school the next year, recycling bins sat outside every classroom. "I thought to myself, 'I did that!'" Julia exclaims.

She's happy to report that her school now recycles more than 250 pounds of paper per week. "It makes me proud."

MANATEE MISSION

When Isabel D. was figuring out what present to get for her friend Gabe's birthday, she wasn't thinking about a new video game or race car. Isabel got Gabe a manatee!

Gabe loves the friendly underwater creatures, and he had shown Isabel a Web site that lets visitors "adopt" manatees by sending money to help pay for their protection.

As Isabel did research for Gabe's gift, she learned that there are only about 3,000 manatees left in the United States and decided that she wanted to help more manatees. "I saw how endangered manatees are and how they're sometimes ignored," says the Pennsylvania girl.

So she and Gabe formed a Save the Manatee Club at school to raise money to adopt more manatees. "We had a goal of adopting seven manatees, but we didn't think we'd even make it to one," admits Isabel, age 11.

Isabel and Gabe did a presentation about manatees and used the school's PA system to talk about the creatures. "You need to spread awareness," Isabel advises. "If nobody knows about your cause, they won't care."

The club organized coin drives. It also sold manatee-themed products, such as T-shirts. All told, the school raised enough to adopt 16 manatees—more than twice the club's goal!

"It felt really great," Isabel says. "My school helped make a big difference!"

Adopting an Endangered Animal

Ask an adult to help you adopt an endangered animal online. Go to www.worldwildlife.org/species/specieslist.html. Or, to adopt an animal in our national zoo in Washington, D.C., go to http://nationalzoo.si.edu/Support/AdoptSpecies.

A manatee mom nurses her calf

In addition to the two Lanie books, Jane Kurtz has written more than 25 books for young readers, including *Saba: Under the Hyena's Foot* for American Girl. Many of her books have won awards, including the middle-grade novel *The Storyteller's Beads* and the picture book *River Friendly, River Wild.*

Ms. Kurtz spent her childhood in Ethiopia, where she spent much of her time outdoors—and where her father had a large vegetable garden! She and her husband now live in Kansas, which is also the home of Monarch Watch, a program focused on monarch butterfly research.

Along with her own writing, Ms. Kurtz teaches about writing, both in the United States and abroad.